Ahoy there, kids! Ready to sing the SpongeBob SquarePants theme song?

I can't hear you!

OOOOOOOOOOOOOOOOOH,

Who lives in a pineapple under the sea?

SpongeBob SquarePants!

Absorbent and yellow and porous is he.

SpongeBob SquarePants!

If nautical nonsense be something you wish,

SpongeBob SquarePants!

Then drop on the deck and flop like a fish.

SpongeBob SquarePants!

SpongeBob SquarePants!

SpongeBob SquarePants!

SpongeBob SquarePants!

Sponge- Bob, Square- Pants!

Ah ha ha

Based on the TV series *SpongeBob SquarePants*®
created by Stephen Hillenburg as seen on Nickelodeon®

SIMON SPOTLIGHT
An imprint of Simon & Schuster Children's Publishing Division
1230 Avenue of the Americas, New York, New York 10020

Manufactured in the United States of America

First Edition
20 19 18 17 16 15 14 13

ISBN 0-689-84194-9

Library of Congress Control Number 00-111807

SpongeBob NaturePants

by Terry Collins

illustrated by Clint Bond

based on the original teleplay by
Peter Burns, Paul Tibbitt, and Mark O'Hare

Simon Spotlight/Nickelodeon

New York London Toronto Sydney Singapore

chapter one

Another day, another juicy, mouth-watering, charbroiled Krabby Patty.

Normally such a sight would make SpongeBob SquarePants beam with pride. Today all he could do was sigh as he gazed down at the same old patties cooking on top of the same old greasy grill. As head fry cook at the famous Krusty Krab fast-food restaurant, SpongeBob spent most of his time behind a hot stove preparing delicious meals for the finny inhabitants of Bikini Bottom.

And what did he get in return? Minimum wage and a 10 percent employee discount.

Taking his spatula, he pressed one of the patties down with a sizzle.

Until recently that sound had made his heart fill with joy, for SpongeBob took his job very seriously.

But not today.

Today the sizzle sounded like work.

Boring old job. Boring old life.

SpongeBob's eyelids drooped. He yawned, then began to hum a sailor's hornpipe tune while trying to keep himself awake. His mind wandered, and he thought of a life outside the kitchen of the Krusty Krab. A life free of Krabby Patties and responsibilities.

SpongeBob looked around the shipshape kitchen of the Krusty Krab, and his stare fell on the single porthole that revealed the great green sea outside.

SpongeBob's mind wandered. He could choose any path he wished—after all, this was *his* daydream. He let his mind start to drift. Next stop—

Ding!

The timer went off! Time to turn the Krabby Patties before they burned on the grill.

SpongeBob flipped the first patty upward with a twist of his wrist, and the delicious treat spun like a top, hanging in midair over the grill . . . and then, before his eyes, the same patty magically changed into a light purple and pink jellyfish!

The jellyfish hovered, buzzed, and waggled its many long tentacles at SpongeBob.

SpongeBob waved back.

After turning a trio of loops, the jellyfish

swam toward the open porthole . . . and then disappeared into the great green beyond of the ocean!

A chant of "Join us, SpongeBob" echoed throughout the kitchen.

"Who is that?" SpongeBob asked, seeking out the voices. "Where are you?"

Pop!

Pop, pop, pop!

Poppity-pop, pop, pop!

SpongeBob looked down at his grill in disbelief as each of the remaining eight patties sprang up and turned into jellyfish! The kitchen was soon filled with their buzzing sounds.

The mass of jellyfish bobbed and weaved in tight formation as they swam around the awestruck SpongeBob.

Then, one by one, they zipped through the porthole . . . and SpongeBob was alone again.

"I wish, I wish, I wish," SpongeBob said. "I wish I were . . . a jellyfish!"

Just then SpongeBob began to rise from the floor of the kitchen, his skinny legs dangling beneath his square pants as he floated past the refrigerator. He drifted, turned a full somersault, and then dove through the porthole after his friends.

SpongeBob was no more. He was now JellyBob!

"Follow me! I know the way," JellyBob said to the group.

Buzz! Buzz! Buzz!

JellyBob closed his eyes, drifting to and fro as the current carried him merrily along. He was free at last!

"SpongeBob?"

Buzz?

"SpongeBob!"

THE
KRUSTY
KRAB

JellyBob frowned and closed his eyes even tighter. Who dared interrupt his patrol of the Jellyfish Fields?

"SpongeBob! Wake up, boy!" Mr. Krabs cried.

"Huh?" SpongeBob asked as he opened his eyes.

The Jellyfish Fields had vanished, along with all of the jellyfish.

The gray kitchen was back.

The smell of the sea reeds was gone, replaced by the scent of smoke in the air.

"Snap to, boy!" Mr. Krabs yelled. "Yer burnin' me money!"

SpongeBob looked at the grill and found it was covered not in Krabby Patties, but in red and yellow flames and black patties burning to a crisp!

chapter two

"GAAAAHHH!" SpongeBob screamed, taking in the sight of the grill in flames.

Throwing up his arms in a panic, SpongeBob fled to safety, hiding behind Mr. Krabs's ample back. His jellyfish fantasy was now forgotten and replaced with the hot reality of a four-alarm fire!

"Mr. Krabs, w-w-what'll we do?" SpongeBob asked.

"What do you mean, 'we?' This is your

show, SpongeBob!" Mr. Krabs replied, grabbing a bright red fire extinguisher off the wall and handing it to his employee. "Here! Use this!"

SpongeBob hefted the canister over his head and, with a grunt, hurled it toward the grill.

Clunk! The extinguisher bounced off the stove.

Before Mr. Krabs could scold SpongeBob, the fire took on a new life, erupting across the top of the stove and covering the counters in hot flames. With a *whoosh* the blaze spread, growing in size and power.

In a matter of seconds, the scene had gone from being a simple grease fire to a major inferno. The intense heat of the flames caused Mr. Krabs to break out in a sweat, even from across the kitchen.

"Hot, hot, hot!" Mr. Krabs shouted. "Oh, but I hate a fire! Makes me outer shell feel extra crunchy!"

SpongeBob looked upon the scene in horror, wincing as the walls began to catch on fire from the blazing grill. Visions of the entire Krusty Krab burning to the ground flashed through SpongeBob's fevered brain. If SpongeBob toasted the restaurant, Mr. Krabs would fire him for sure!

One thing was for certain—SpongeBob was no longer bored on the job.

"This is my fault," SpongeBob said as he hitched up his square pants. There was a determined gleam in his eye. "I'll take care of the problem."

SpongeBob approached the blazing grill. Taking a deep breath, he began to huff and puff in an effort to blow out the fire. However, instead of blowing out the flames, his efforts only fanned them into a brighter bonfire!

"That's not working, SpongeBob!" Mr. Krabs called. "Back off before you get cooked yerself!"

"Must . . . stop . . . fire!" SpongeBob panted, huffing and puffing even harder.

"Could I get an order of fries and a chocolate shake to go—holy smoke!" a voice said.

Mr. Krabs spun around to find a fireman standing in the doorway of the kitchen.

"The kitchen's closed, but I'll give you a 10 percent discount coupon if you'll put out that blaze!" Mr. Krabs said.

"Deal! I'll fetch my hose!" the fireman agreed, racing out of the blazing kitchen.

"Stand back, SpongeBob!" Mr. Krabs called. "Help is on the way!"

Sploosh! A blast of water shot out toward the burning kitchen, but SpongeBob was standing in the way. As he spun to see what was going on, he caught the water right in the mouth.

"Urgle! Gurgle! Blub!" SpongeBob gargled.

As the pressure of the hose blasted more and more water into SpongeBob's mouth, his head began to grow. The more water the fireman sprayed, the more SpongeBob's head puffed up like a water balloon at a carnival game.

"Move out of the way!" Mr. Krabs called. "You're soaking up all the water!"

SpongeBob began to wobble on his feet.

Splat! He splashed heavily on the burning stovetop. With a loud *ssssssssss*, his wet body extinguished the flames.

Though it would need a good airing out and fresh wallpaper, the kitchen was saved.

"Hooray!" the fireman cried.

"Your discount coupon," Mr. Krabs announced, giving the fireman a certificate. "Eat in good health!"

As the fireman rolled up his hose, Mr. Krabs stepped over to SpongeBob. He was still flat on his back on top of the now-cool grill. SpongeBob's head had returned to normal size, although he was covered from head to foot in soot from the burnt Krabby Patties.

Mr. Krabs cracked his claws and picked up SpongeBob's dropped spatula, using the tool to scrape his slightly dazed employee off the range.

"SpongeBob," Mr. Krabs announced as he flipped the spatula over one shoulder. "Come into me office."

chapter three

"What's wrong, me boy?" Mr. Krabs asked as he gazed across the top of the sea chest he used as a desk. "This isn't like you at all, nearly burning down the place."

"Well, I-I . . . ," SpongeBob stammered, his eyes darting around the office.

"This is the fourth time this week I've had to scrape you offa somethin'!" Mr. Krabs said, waving the spatula. "That's no way to run a kitchen, Head Fry Cook SpongeBob!"

SpongeBob gazed up at his boss. "Well, I've been thinking."

Mr. Krabs squished the tip of his claw into SpongeBob's forehead. "We need to get you thinkin' about *work!*"

"No offense, Mr. Krabs," SpongeBob replied, choosing his words carefully. "But I've been thinking about giving up my cold industrial life here in Bikini Bottom in favor of a more natural and free life among the jellyfish."

The crab's eyes pivoted on their elongated stalks as he peered at SpongeBob.

"Ah, gah-gah-gah-ha-ha!" Mr. Krabs laughed, his wide red body shaking with glee. "Oh, SpongeBob, you wouldn't last even one day in the wild. You are what we crabs call *domesticated.*"

"Come, follow me," Mr. Krabs announced, striding from his desk and heading for the restaurant's kitchen. SpongeBob did as he was told, walking behind the restaurant owner.

"This is your natural habitat!" Mr. Krabs said, spreading his arms open wide and gesturing for SpongeBob to take in the entire sight. "These walls, that stove—all yours!"

The crab strolled over to the blackened grill. "This is your wide-open range!" he announced with a flourish.

Mr. Krabs led SpongeBob past the baskets of fries cooking in the grease pits. "These are your amber waves!" he said.

Working his way up to his dramatic conclusion, Mr. Krabs held up SpongeBob's spatula like a knight brandishing his sword. "And this . . . ohhhh, this is your golden scepter! This is what you rule the kitchen with!"

Mr. Krabs wiped his brow. "Now," he said, "that's better than nasty ol' jellyfish, right, SpongeBob?"

Silence.

Mr. Krabs turned to find he was alone in the kitchen.

Outside the Krusty Krab, SpongeBob stood and looked at the front doors of the restaurant. "I can *too* last more than one day," he muttered. "I'll show him! I'll show them all!"

SpongeBob reached up and removed his sacred badge of office, the official Krusty Krab Captain's Cap, and threw it to the ground.

"Awwww, barnacles!" he cried, stomping down the street. "I quit!"

Mr. Krabs burst through the front doors. "SpongeBob, wait!" he called. But SpongeBob was already gone.

"Oh, he'll be back all right," Mr. Krabs said in a confident voice as he looked down and spotted SpongeBob's abandoned cap. "He'll be back. . . ."

chapter four

After arriving at his pineapple home, SpongeBob gathered up an armload of his worldly possessions and walked out into the front yard. Calling his neighbors over, he began to give away everything he owned.

"I don't care what he wants to give me," Squidward chortled. "As long as he's gone!"

Standing before SpongeBob, Squidward held up a tentacle and waved bye-bye.

"Squidward," SpongeBob announced, reaching

into a bag. "I want *you* to have my can opener!"

Squidward took the rusty kitchen tool. The can opener wasn't even electric.

"For me?" Squidward said, rolling his eyes sarcastically. "Gee, and I thought this friendship would never pay off."

"Enjoy! I have no further use for such things," SpongeBob replied.

Patrick Star, SpongeBob's best friend, raced back to the head of the line.

"Are-are-are you *sure* you wanna give me this jar of mayonnaise?" he babbled, clasping the half-empty jar to one cheek like a baby.

SpongeBob shrugged and grinned. "It's all yours!"

Patrick put the jar down and lifted up his other gift. "And these old phone books?" he asked, his entire body quivering with emotion.

"For you, and you alone, old friend." SpongeBob beamed.

"I'll trade you my can opener," Squidward muttered.

"Oh, wait. Patrick, there is one more thing I want you to have," SpongeBob called as he took out a long wooden box. He flipped open the lid and a golden glow flooded everyone's eyes.

Patrick was flabbergasted as he peered at the gift within. "Wow! Ol' Reliable!"

SpongeBob took out the prize fishing net and handed it over to Patrick.

"Yes, well, I doubt I'll be doing much in the way of jellyfish hunting what with my new lifestyle choice and all," SpongeBob said.

Patrick gave the net a few practice swings. "It's beautiful," he said.

Sandy Cheeks, SpongeBob's squirrel friend, walked up. "Howdy, y'all!" she said, taking in

MAYO

the scene of the big giveaway.

"Hi, Sandy," SpongeBob replied. "Want some toothpaste?"

"No, thanks," the squirrel chuckled. "What's up? You havin' a garage sale?"

"No, Sandy, I'm giving up my material possessions to live in the wild with the jellyfish," SpongeBob replied. "Buzz, buzz! That's the life for me!"

"Of all the crazy schemes!" Sandy scolded. "Why would you wanna live among jellyfish? They're cold and mean and none too bright!"

SpongeBob reached over and patted the top of Sandy's air helmet. "That's exactly the response I would expect from someone who lives the sham of a life I once lived," he said. "I'm going to prove that I don't need all this stuff to be happy. Maybe someday you'll wise up and join me."

"Humph!" Sandy retorted as SpongeBob gave his friends a wave.

"Good-bye!" he said as he walked briskly toward the hills where Jellyfish Fields was hidden.

SpongeBob stopped. He reached down and, with one quick motion, stripped off his square pants and dropped them next to a bush. "Guess I won't be needing these!" he announced. "Well, time to brush up on the local language. Buzz, buzz, buzz, buzz!"

The trio watched their buzzing friend race away without his clothing.

"Patrick SAD!" the starfish wailed, falling to his knees and pounding the ground with his fists.

"He . . . he took off his pants," Squidward said in disbelief, watching as Patrick wept over SpongeBob's abandoned pair of trousers.

"I give him a week," Sandy said, shaking her head.

chapter five

SpongeBob stood silently, looking across a valley filled with dozens of floating jellyfish. A warning sign reading CAUTION: JELLYFISH FIELDS had been nailed to a post.

"I . . . I'm home," SpongeBob whispered, caressing the wooden front of the sign.

SpongeBob tried to contain himself but couldn't hold back his enthusiasm. Racing into the fields, he started chanting, "I'm home! I'm home! I'm home!"

As he ran up to greet the jellyfish, they zipped away, vanishing inside a large brown hive hanging high above the fields.

"Brothers and sisters, wait for me!" SpongeBob cried, running after the group. "Buzz, buzz, buzz!"

Zoom! The umbrella-shaped jellyfish flew out of the hive, leaving a trail of bubbles in their wake.

"Okay, buzz, buzz! I'm here!" SpongeBob said as he ran after them. "Now, let's start—buzz, buzz, buzz—doing some jellyfish stuff!"

Zip! Once again, the jellyfish swam away.

SpongeBob ran after them again, waving his spindly arms. "Wait! No! I just got settled!" he cried, watching them hover near a large clump of glowing green seaweed.

As SpongeBob watched, the swarm of jellyfish spun around the seaweed, gobbling up the entire plant in a matter of seconds!

"Ahhhhh," SpongeBob said. "Food for us jellyfish-type persons!"

Spying his own supply of seaweed growing from the ocean floor, SpongeBob reached over and ripped up a clump. "Buzz, buzz, buzz!" he said as he popped the seaweed into his mouth.

SpongeBob chewed vigorously and gave a wide smile to his new kin, his teeth stained bright green from the seaweed.

"Ahh! Mmmm! This is the life!" he said. "Buzz, buzz, buzz!"

Then the flavor of what he was eating began to sink into his taste buds.

Squishing between his teeth was a gob of cold, damp, wet seaweed . . . and it tasted horrible!

"Nyuueuh!" SpongeBob said, sticking out his tongue. A wad of half-chewed goo was stuck to the roof of his mouth. Gagging, he spit the chewed seaweed out and used his hands to scrape away the remains of his underwater salad.

"Blech!" SpongeBob said with a shudder. "Mental note: Next time, try another bush."

He looked around for his new pals and saw the gang of jellyfish gathered in rows, floating peacefully back and forth as they drifted in unison.

"Buzz, buzz, nice current today!" SpongeBob said as he stepped over and greeted the group.

The jellyfish didn't answer.

"Hey, what's the buzz?" SpongeBob asked one of the jellyfish on the end of a row. He stuck out a hand for a friendly shake. "Hello, I'm JellyBob! And you are? . . . "

The jellyfish floated up a tentacle in reply, which SpongeBob took and shook.

Zortch! A stinging shock arced from the stingers on the tentacle to SpongeBob's hand!

Foomp! SpongeBob's hand swelled to ten times its normal size and began to pulsate,

Jellyfish
Fields

changing color back and forth from pale yellow to bright cherry red. His friendly face twisted in pain as he tried to grin at his new friend.

"Heh. Nice to meet you, too," SpongeBob said, his voice trailing off as his nose started to wiggle. A new smell had invaded the Jellyfish Fields, one that SpongeBob knew quite well.

"Mmmm!" he murmured as he followed his nose around a grassy knoll. Climbing to the top, SpongeBob looked down and spied Patrick and Sandy.

His former chums were seated comfortably on a red and white checkered tablecloth having a picnic. And stacked on a plate between them was the source of the scent SpongeBob had sniffed—a heaping helping of Krabby Patties!

Catching sight of SpongeBob out of the corner of her eye, Sandy said, "Here, Patrick. Have a Krabby Patty!"

Patrick gave Sandy a blank stare as a reply.

"SpongeBob's here, Patrick," she whispered. "That's your cue to say your line."

Patrick took out the script Sandy had written. "Why-thank-you-Sandy. I-would-love-one," he read in a stiff voice.

"That's terrible!" Sandy whispered, trying to look inconspicuous. "Put some life into it!"

"Duh, um, take-Patty," Patrick said.

"No, no!" Sandy groaned. "That's one of the stage directions. Don't read those!"

Patrick continued to read, his eyes welling with tears. "Too-bad-Sponge-Bob-isn't-here, these-are-his-favorites. I-sure-wish-he'd-come-home. Take-bite."

"That's another stage direction," Sandy hissed.

"I . . . I can't do it!" Patrick wailed, tossing his script over his head and spinning to face SpongeBob. "SpongeBob! Come home!"

chapter six

SpongeBob looked down from the top of the grassy knoll at Sandy and Patrick. He frowned and crossed his arms in defiance. "Patrick, I'm not coming back," he said. "The wide open spaces of the wild are where I live now."

"But I miss you!" Patrick cried. "I miss you lots!"

Sandy gave a small wave. Patrick pointed at the squirrel. "See! Sandy misses you too!"

Gary, SpongeBob's pet snail, poked his

eyes out from inside the picnic basket. "Meow?" he said, awakened by Patrick's voice.

"Look! Look!" Patrick said, snatching up the snail and hefting it toward SpongeBob. "Even Gary misses you."

"I'm happy here. This is my new home!" SpongeBob said, turning on his heel and walking away. "Now, please . . . leave me alone. Good-bye!"

"NOOOOOOOOOOOO!" Patrick screamed, beating the ground with his fists.

Sandy looked down at Patrick. "It's no use. We'll try again later," she said. "Come on. Let's go."

Patrick wasn't listening. He continued to call for his friend.

"SPOOOOONGEBOB!" Patrick bellowed. "I'm not giving up on you, buddy! You'll see!"

Sandy shrugged and began the long walk back to Bikini Bottom. "Those two deserve one another," she muttered.

Meanwhile, back in the midst of Jellyfish Fields, SpongeBob once again attempted to bond with the pack of invertebrates.

"Hey, everybody! I'm back!" he said happily, wiggling his long legs and arms like tentacles. "Check me out! I think I'm getting the hang of this!"

In response, the jellyfish scattered in all directions, leaving behind a droopy and disappointed SpongeBob. How was he going to make a connection?

Swish! Water churned past SpongeBob's cheek as a net narrowly missed plopping down on his head. He spun to find a crazed Patrick staring him in the face.

"Hello!" Patrick said. He had given up on asking SpongeBob to return. With the help of Ol' Reliable, the very same net SpongeBob had once given him, Patrick was taking matters into his own hands.

"Patrick! W-what are you doing?" SpongeBob asked as he slowly inched away.

"If I can't have you as a friend . . . I'm gonna make you into a trophy!" the wild-eyed starfish replied. He held up a glass specimen jar labeled SPONGEBOB—FRIEND. "See! I even picked out this nice jar for you."

"Patrick! Go home! I'm a jellyfish now!" SpongeBob cried.

Patrick whimpered and bit his lower lip as he screwed off the lid of the jar. Holding it out to SpongeBob, he gestured for the sponge to climb inside. "Go on, get in!" he urged.

"Ummm, I don't think so, Patrick," SpongeBob said.

"Fine!" Patrick snorted, tossing the jar over his shoulder. He beat his chest with his fleshy fists, grabbed up Ol' Reliable, and unleashed the mighty war cry of the warrior starfish clan!

"AAUUUUGHAHAHOZOOOOGHAAH! AUGHHOOOHAUOOUH-HOO!" he bellowed as he swung the net. SpongeBob dodged, then turned tail and ran as fast as his squeaky shoes would carry him.

Searching for cover, SpongeBob spied a hiding place. He dove behind a large blue rock and wiped his brow. He was safe . . . until the rock sprouted eyes, meowed once, and slowly crawled away.

SpongeBob groaned. It was just his luck to use a giant snail as a hiding place.

"I can see you there!" Patrick called.

SpongeBob got to his feet and ran over to a coral cluster.

"I can *still* see you!" Patrick said.

Picking a large sea bush, SpongeBob hid a

third time, but there was no stopping his pursuer.

"You're gonna look good on my mantle!" Patrick leered, bringing down Ol' Reliable and nearly netting his spongy prey. "Friends forever, SpongeBob!"

SpongeBob lunged from hiding place to hiding place but could not shake Patrick's dogged determination to capture him. Still, he kept a lead over the slower starfish, until fate tossed a pebble in his path and caused him to trip.

SpongeBob rolled over to find Patrick standing over him in triumph. The starfish was twirling Ol' Reliable in both hands.

"I got you now, SpongeBob!" he said with a giggle. "I got you now!"

chapter seven

"Nowhere left to go," SpongeBob gasped as he braced himself for capture.

Then the sponge saw his sanctuary.

Summoning up the last reserves of his strength, SpongeBob dodged the net and leapt upward toward the hanging hive of the jellyfish!

Thoomp! SpongeBob plunged headfirst into the entrance hole of the hive. It was a tight fit, but with some straining, he was able to pull himself safely within.

Below, Patrick gasped in shock. Then he got mad, stomping his feet and shaking his fists at the now-secure SpongeBob. There was no way the chubby starfish would ever fit into the hive. In fact, he couldn't even jump high enough to try.

Again and again, Patrick leaped up and swung his net, but the hive remained safely out of his reach.

"Okay! So this is the way it's gonna be, huh?" he called up to SpongeBob. "I hope you're happy!"

Snap! Patrick broke Ol' Reliable over his knee and stomped away.

SpongeBob watched Patrick leave. "Well, that's over with!" he said with relief. "Now, back to jellyfish matters."

As SpongeBob readied himself to get out of the hive, a dollop of light purple jelly dripped

down from the ceiling and landed on the tip of his nose.

SpongeBob sniffed the glob. "Mmmmm! Jelly!" he said.

The jelly smelled delicious, and he was *very* hungry . . . so he stuck his finger in the goo and gave it a taste.

"Yum!" SpongeBob proclaimed, and he began to shovel the jelly into his mouth with both hands. As he gobbled up the goop, his face and hands were coated with a sticky purple film.

Then he heard a familiar buzz.

"Ah! My jellyfish brethren are—buzz buzz—returning!" SpongeBob said happily.

"Buzzzzzzz," replied the jellyfish as they approached the hive.

The gang of jellyfish flew into the hive, and SpongeBob gave a jaunty wave. "Greetings, comrades!" he said with a smile.

The jellyfish hovered, surrounding the new inhabitant of their hive. With SpongeBob squeezed inside the chamber, the interior of their home was very crowded.

Too crowded.

From outside the hive all was quiet . . . until a series of bright white flashes erupted from within, along with the snap and crackle of unleashed electricity.

Zortch! Zap! Zark!

The hive began to vibrate, jiggling back and forth. Faster and faster the hive shook, until SpongeBob's head popped out of the entrance.

"YAAAAAAAAA!" he screamed as the jellyfish stung him over and over.

Zap! Zortch! Zark!

"Gangway!" SpongeBob yelled, pulling

himself free of the hive, falling to the ground, and racing away.

The swarm of jellyfish buzzed at his heels, stinging SpongeBob over and over! SpongeBob flapped his arms and tried to shoo the creatures away as they zapped and stung *every* part of his spongy yellow body.

"Ow! Ow! Ouch! Ooh! Ow!" SpongeBob cried at each new sting. He ran for the border of the fields, away from the painful stings, away from the mean jellyfish—and away from the life he had imagined for himself.

With his skin on fire from the stinging tentacles of the jellyfish, *and* from the even more painful sting of rejection, SpongeBob ran past the CAUTION: JELLYFISH FIELDS sign and never looked back.

chapter eight

The deep blue of night arrived on the ocean floor.

After driving SpongeBob from their midst, the horde of jellyfish had given up the chase. Exhausted and disappointed by the day's events, SpongeBob had found refuge within a cold, dank cave.

Now he was alone and sitting on the floor of his new home—a sponge without a country.

"Gee, being a jellyfish sure was fun," SpongeBob

said in a defeated whisper. "Buzz. Buzz, buzz, buzz."

SpongeBob looked down at himself. His entire body was riddled with red welts, throbbing leftovers from the multiple stings.

What had he learned today?

"For one thing, never, *ever* eat jellyfish jelly out of the hive," SpongeBob declared. His teeth started to chatter from the cool of the night, and a chill went down his back. The gloom of the cave had settled in his bones, and he began to shiver.

SpongeBob peeled off a sheet of moss from a nearby wall and spread it over his body like a blanket. He lay down flat on his back and stared up at the roof of the cave.

However, the mossy blanket was too short and kept rolling up like a broken window shade, exposing his ankles to the cold. Try as he might, SpongeBob could not get comfortable. He tried using a rock as a pillow, but it gave him a headache.

SpongeBob sighed. He missed his nice soft bed back inside his pineapple in Bikini Bottom.

He closed his eyes and dreamed of home.

Then his back began to itch.

SpongeBob popped up into a sitting position and scratched with both hands.

"Hey! Ooh! I'm itchy! Itchy!" he cried. "Why am I so itchy?"

SpongeBob pulled away his blanket to reveal dozens of tiny orange buglike creatures crawling on his body.

"Poison sea urchins!" SpongeBob gasped. "AHHHH!"

Springing to his feet, SpongeBob tried to brush the invaders away, but they were too stubborn to move. He rubbed his back against

a stalactite, but the urchins still held fast. In a panic, he ran from the cave and threw himself down on the soft sand of the ocean floor, wiggling on his stomach and face like an inchworm.

"Itch! Ahh! Itch! Ow! Ow! Itch!"

The grit of the sand loosened the hold of the clinging critters and gave SpongeBob some quick relief. Unfortunately, now his skin ached from the jellyfish stings *and* from the bites of the tiny urchins.

SpongeBob stood up and hung his head in shame.

What was he going to do? Where was he going to go?

For now, he picked a direction and walked. Away from the unknown and toward the familiar. Off in the distance he could see the skyline of Bikini Bottom.

As he passed the city limits sign, SpongeBob gave a feeble "buzz." His dreams of being a jellyfish seemed silly now as he walked down the deserted streets of his hometown. There was the Library of Oceanography, the Salty Snail Disco, and, off the corner of Fin Lane and Gill Street, the Krusty Krab Restaurant.

A CLOSED sign hung on the front doors. SpongeBob stepped up to the darkened windows and peered inside. He pressed his face to the glass and squinted at the empty tables, the stacked menus, and a platter of leftover Krabby Patties sitting on the counter.

SpongeBob's tongue lolled out of his mouth. He licked the glass in frustration.

"Krabby Patties," he mumbled.

More dejected than ever, SpongeBob continued on his lonely walk.

He passed Sandy's treedome. Like the

Krusty Krab, the squirrel's home was also dark.

"Sandy," SpongeBob sobbed. "Oh, Sandy!"

SpongeBob kept walking, his feet taking him toward his own street by habit.

There was Patrick's rock and, next door, Squidward's two-story tiki house.

"Patrick, old friend," SpongeBob sighed. "Squidward, buddy, ol' pal!"

And finally he arrived before the last house on the lane, his very own orange pineapple palace.

SpongeBob stood at his front door. "What have I done?" he wailed. "I had a great life and friends, and I . . . I gave all of that up!"

Still, since he was here, perhaps he'd take a little peek. SpongeBob carefully swung open the door and peered inside the darkened room. . . .

chapter nine

"SURPRISE!"

SpongeBob staggered back in shock as a loud cry of voices erupted from within his living room. The lights popped on, and there, waiting for him, were all of his friends!

Sandy and Patrick blew on noisemakers.

Mr. Krabs waved a pennant.

Even Squidward wore a purple party hat.

SpongeBob gaped at the sight. The living room was festooned with colorful streamers and a huge WELCOME HOME, SPONGEBOB! banner. Balloons hung from the ceiling and furniture. Punch and cookies and a stack of hot Krabby Patties were waiting on a table.

"About time you showed up!" Mr. Krabs called. "I knew you couldn't resist the civilized world!"

SpongeBob stepped into the room. "You guys are the best!" he said, his voice cracking with joy. "I made a huge mistake in leaving! Please forgive me."

"Ah, quit yer blubberin' and have a Krabby Patty!" Mr. Krabs said.

"Don't mind if I do!" SpongeBob replied, taking a big bite and savoring the flavor. A Krabby Patty beat out a mouthful of seaweed anytime!

Mr. Krabs reached into his pocket and removed an official Krusty Krab Captain's Cap. "And I'll see you at work tomorrow morning!" he said as he placed the headgear on SpongeBob.

SpongeBob snapped off a crisp salute. "Aye, aye, Cap'n!" he said between bites.

Squidward stepped up and handed over SpongeBob's discarded pair of brown square pants.

"SpongeBob," he said. "Do us all a favor and put these back on."

"With pleasure!" SpongeBob replied, taking the pants and squeezing his lower body into them with a loud *snap!*

SpongeBob felt his lip start to quiver. Food, friends, his pants . . . it was all too much for him to take!

"I . . . I'm so happy!" SpongeBob said, lunging forward and wrapping his arms around Squidward. "I can hardly contain myself!"

Squidward scrunched his eyes shut in

discomfort from the surprise hug and waited for SpongeBob to let go. Ten seconds passed. Twenty.

"Ooookay, that's enough," Squidward said, trying to free himself.

Unfortunately for Squidward, Mr. Krabs, Sandy, and Patrick all wrapped their arms around SpongeBob for a big group hug. Even Gary came out of his shell.

"Ahhhhh!" the group breathed.

"Ick," Squidward added, hoping no one brought a camera.

"Meow!" Gary said.

"Could we please, *please* stop this," Squidward begged. "I'm allergic to affection."

Squidward's request was granted as the group let go all at once. Everyone but SpongeBob wore a wide-eyed expression of discomfort and exchanged nervous glances.

Still no one spoke, until Patrick cried out, "Patrick ITCHY!"

On cue, the gang began to frantically scratch their bodies with both hands. When that didn't help, they fell to the floor and began to writhe in a circle, their bodies chugging along like a train of runaway inchworms!

SpongeBob stood in the middle of the circle, looking down on his friends. Apparently, he had brought his *own* surprise to the party. His flat yellow face beamed with contentment.

"It's great to be home!" he said.